"This book is a great first step for helping parents start the conversation about anxiety with their children. Not only does this book normalize these feelings for everyone, but it also gives you the tools to help your child work through these big feelings."

-Robin Drucker, MD, Pediatrician in Palo Alto, CA

"Not only is this children's book delightful and engaging, it is also very timely in addressing the anxiety that all of our children must be feeling."

- Cheryl Fischer, MA, AMFT

"As a school based therapist and clinical supervisor working with students of all ages for over 15 years and having a private practice for teens and adults, the most common challenges I see are related to anxiety. This book normalizes these challenges, invites the reader to seek help if needed and gives a wonderful visualization about how to put down the heavy burden of worry. I can't wait to read this with my clients!"

- Lisa Maggiani-Ayala, LMFT

walking with my elephant

Written by Nicole Marie
Illustrated by Janae Dueck

Dedicated to all the helping hands.
- Nicole

I've always loved walking
Because no matter what the pace is,
Putting one foot in front of the other
Means I'm going places!

Sometimes I take long strides.
They get me moving fast.
Other times I slow down a bit,
To make the journey last.

It doesn't really matter,
Be it quick or slow.
I just love knowing these feet will take me
Exactly where I want to go.

Even when my toes get turned
And lead me way off track,
I simply twist this way or that
To get them moving back.

So, I just keep walking,
Because no matter what the pace is
Putting one foot in front of the other
Means I'm going places!

One day I had been walking,
My destination almost found
When my toes got tangled under me
And I toppled to the ground.

My feet shot up. My head crashed down.
All in between felt twisted and bent.
I'm pretty sure it was right then
I met my elephant.

Since the world seemed unfamiliar
And so much felt upside down,
I was glad Worry rushed over
To help me off the ground!

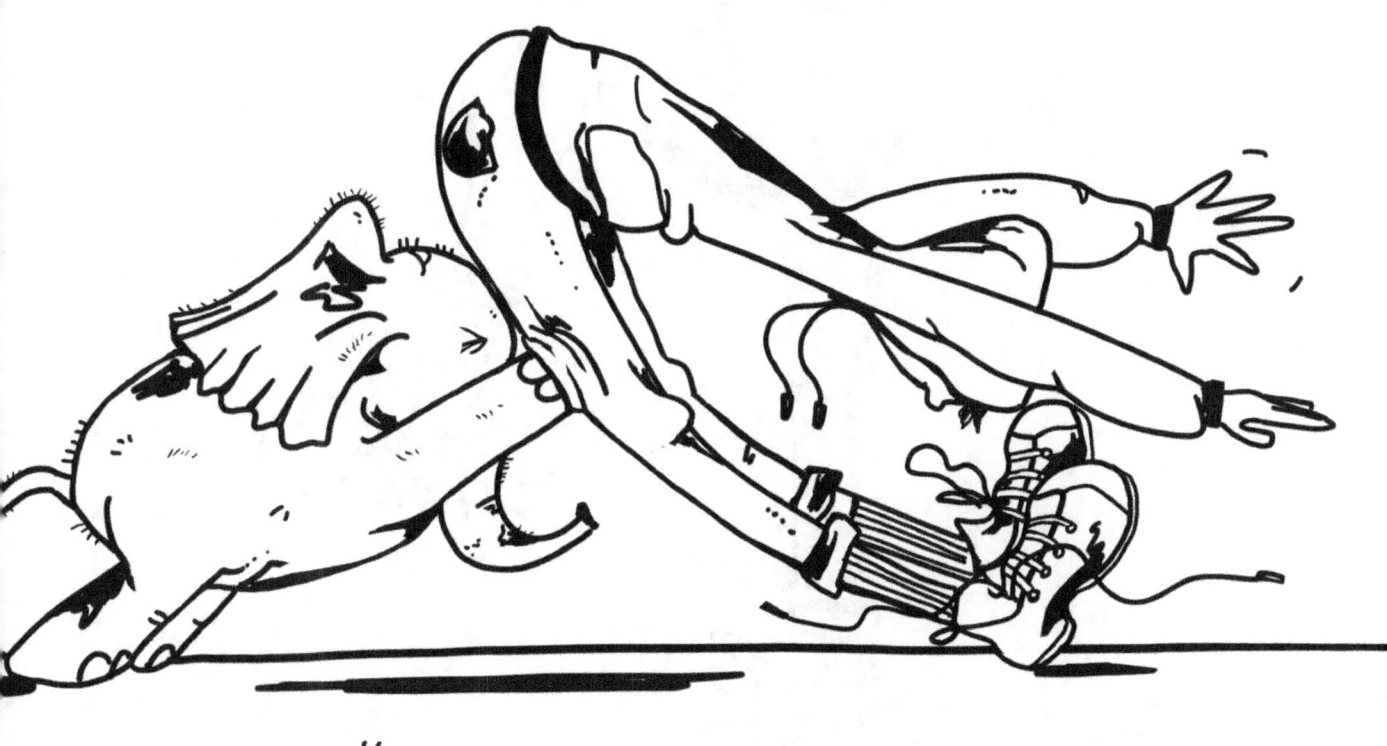

Dusted off and ready,
With Worry by my side
I continued on my journey
Tackling things I'd never tried.

I wanted to keep walking,
But Worry made me slow.
I soon began to question
All the things I **used** to know.

At first I thought it helped me
To have Worry tag along.
But the more he was around,
The more it felt all wrong!

Pretty soon I wasn't walking.
Heck, I could barely crawl.
Carrying an elephant
Wasn't good for me at all!

I used to love walking.
Then my feet got **stuck.**
I kept spinning in one place,
While Worry ran amok!

It was time to trim him down to size,
To show Worry who's in charge.
But, I couldn't tackle him alone,
For he'd gotten far too **large.**

So I reached down deep within,
Held my head high with pride,
I gathered up my courage...
"Help me please!" I cried.

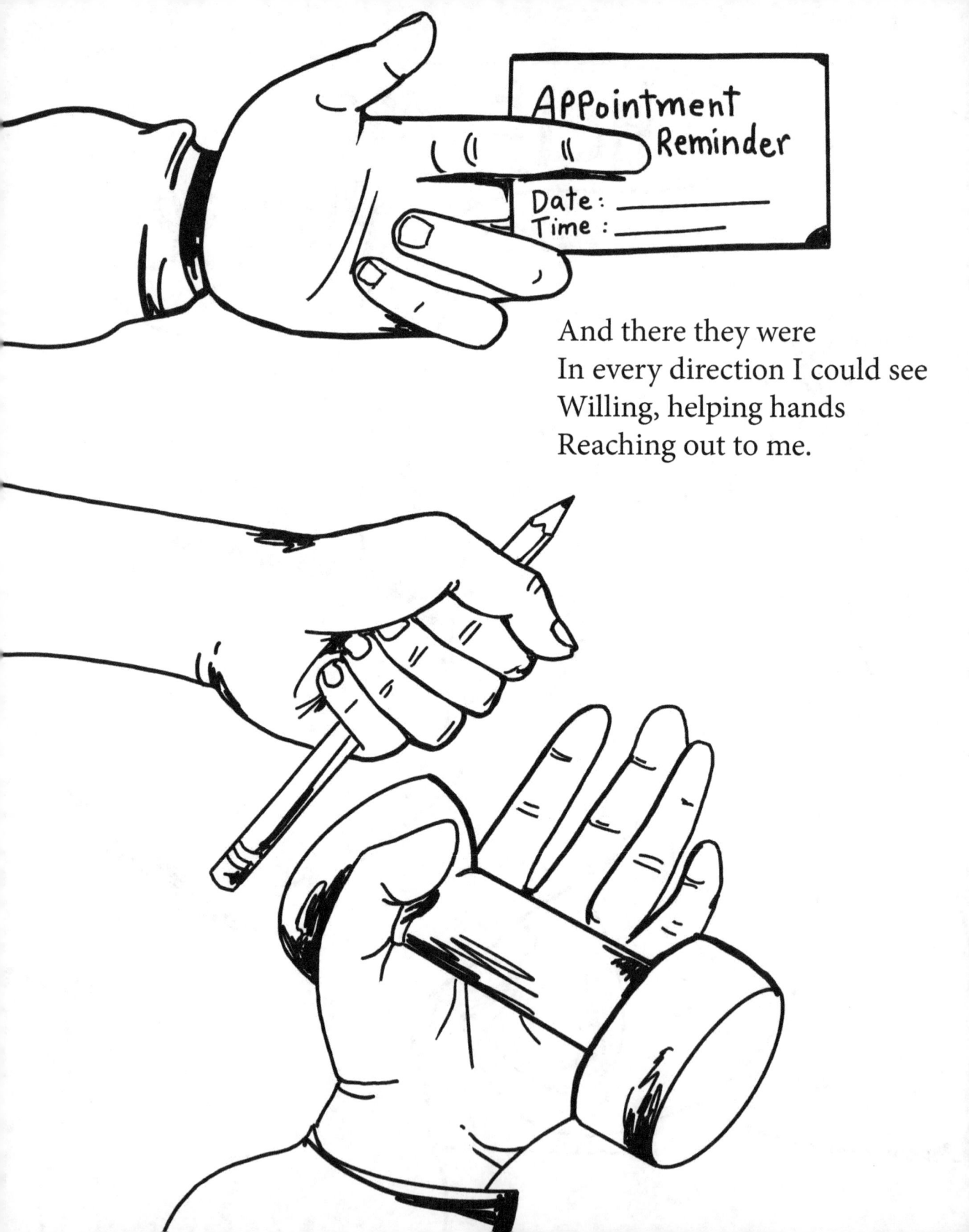

And there they were
In every direction I could see
Willing, helping hands
Reaching out to me.

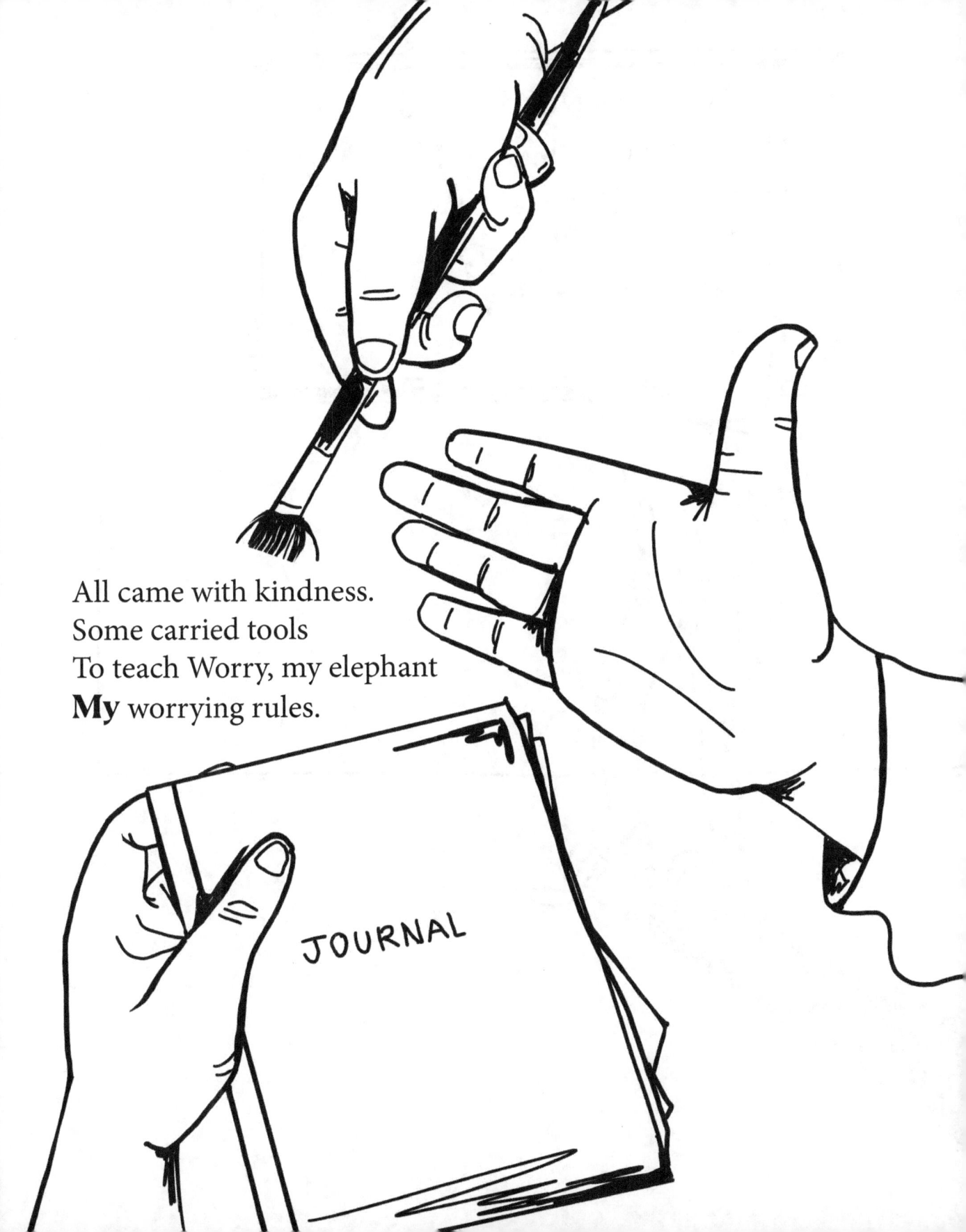

All came with kindness.
Some carried tools
To teach Worry, my elephant
My worrying rules.

They helped me take the reigns,
So Worry couldn't call each shot.
Then I set into motion
A plan that helped a lot.

I would still visit Worry
If a passing need arose.
At times he could be helpful
To keep me on my toes.

But, there'd be no more walking with me.
Worry can't just lurk around.
He must leave with the moment
So he doesn't weigh me down.

It wasn't always easy.
It didn't happen overnight.

But as I put the work in
My goals came into sight.

These days I'm back to walking
And, no matter what the case is
Putting one foot in front of the other
Keeps me going places!

Trim your elephant down to size with these do anytime/any place exercises:

1. **Square Breathing**- Breathe in for four seconds. Hold your breath for four seconds. Breathe out for four seconds. Hold your breath for four seconds. Repeat.

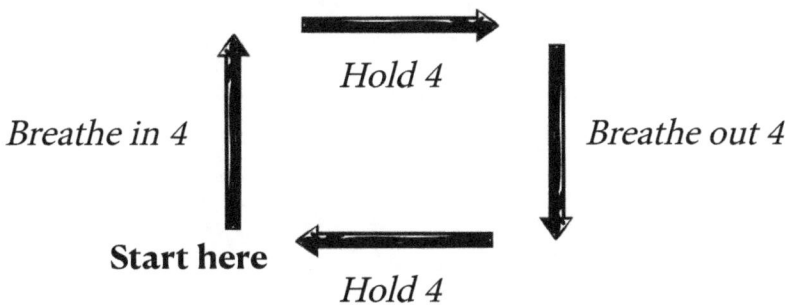

Breathe in 4

Hold 4

Breathe out 4

Start here

Hold 4

2. **Mindfulness Exercise**- In your immediate environment...

Say 5 things you see.
4 things you hear.
3 things you feel or touch.
2 things you smell.
1 thing you taste.

3. **Drop Anchor**- Press your feet into the floor. Notice the floor underneath you. Feel the muscles in your legs tighten. Firmly press your fingertips together, dropping your shoulders and extending your neck. Straighten your back and focus on your body connecting you to the earth.

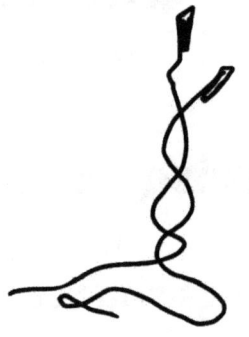

www.ingramcontent.com/pod-product-compliance
Lightning Source LLC
Chambersburg PA
CBHW080836250626
47160CB00008B/2959